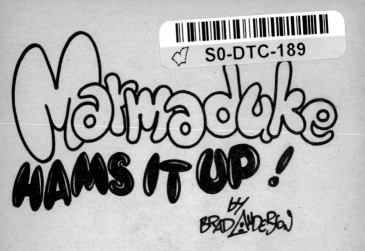

Marmaduke
HAMS IT UP!

by
BRAD ANDERSON

TOR
A TOM DOHERTY ASSOCIATES BOOK

MARMADUKE HAMS IT UP!

First printing: February 1986

A TOR Book

Published by Tom Doherty Associates
49 West 24 Street
New York, N.Y. 10010

Cover art by Brad Anderson

ISBN: 0-812-57346-3

Printed in the United States

0 9 8 7 6 5 4 3 2 1

Look for all these Marmaduke books from Tor

6

9

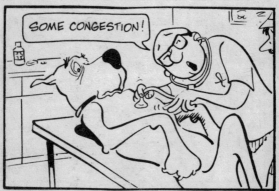

13

9-11

BRADANDERSON

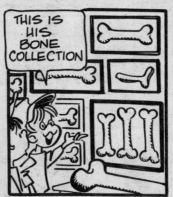

31

11-27

7-25

54

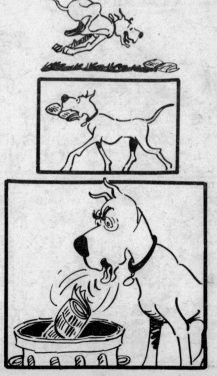

66

67

73

75

83

96

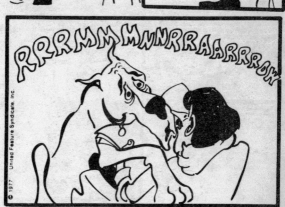

110

3-20

BRAD ANDERSON

123

134

7-24 BRAD ANDERSON

7·27

164

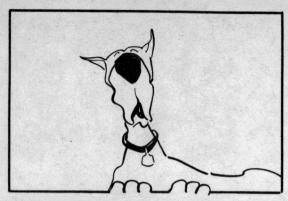

177

Dear Marmaduke:
Jeff Frank of St. Petersburg, Fla. has a 150 lb. Great Dane, "Cricket," who thinks she's a poodle and tries to sit in your lap!

YOU'LL **LOVE** THIS ONE!

PORTLAND, N.Y.
DEAR MARMADUKE:
MY DOG DEE DEE LOVES TO EAT CORN! SHE GOES TO THE GARDEN, PULLS UP A STALK OF CORN AND EATS THE **WHOLE** THING!
— *Jerry Salhoff*

THIS IS PRICELESS!

Dear Marmaduke —
We live in Omaha, Neb., and once had a police dog who consumed a big rump roast I had prepared for my husband while I was away!

Also, we had a young lady spending the night in our downstairs bedroom. Her screams midst a big storm had us falling down the stairs... to find Caesar in bed with her. He was deathly afraid of thunder and lightning!
— *Mrs. L. Holst*

I KNEW YOU WOULD LIKE THOSE!

11-30

205

208

3·1

RING RING

PHIL! IT'S FOR YOU FROM THE DIRECTOR OF THE BOYS' CLUB **FRISBEE TOURNAMENT**

... AND HE SOUNDS MAD!

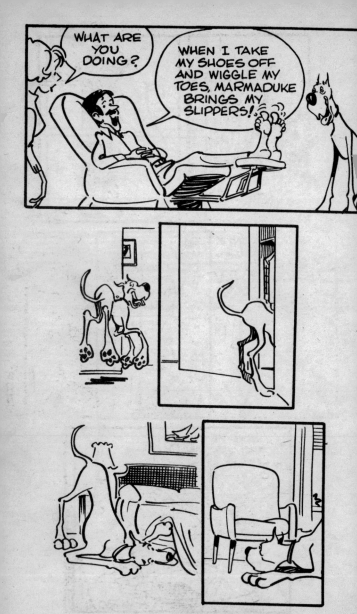

3-8

YOU GOTTA BE KIDDING! THOSE ARE BRONZED *BABY* SHOES!

AW, PHIL... NOW YOU'VE HURT HIS FEELINGS!

NOW HE FEELS BETTER!

YEH! BUT I FEEL SILLY!

223

227

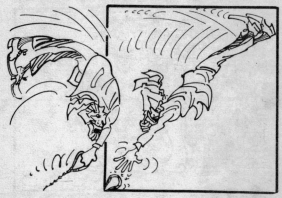

242

243

246

BEETLE BAILEY
THE WACKIEST G.I. IN THE ARMY